# Now You See Me

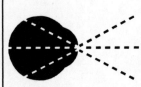

This Large Print Book carries the
Seal of Approval of N.A.V.H.

# Now You See Me

## S. J. Bolton

**WHEELER PUBLISHING**
*A part of Gale, Cengage Learning*

GALE
CENGAGE Learning

Detroit • New York • San Francisco • New Haven, Conn • Waterville, Maine • London

**LIBRARY OF CONGRESS CATALOGING-IN-PUBLICATION DATA**

Bolton, S. J.
  Now you see me / by S. J. Bolton.
    p. cm.
  ISBN-13: 978-1-4104-4138-6 (hardcover)
  ISBN-10: 1-4104-4138-5 (hardcover)
    1. Women detectives—England—London—Fiction. 2. Women—Crimes
against—Fiction. 3. Serial murder investigation—Fiction. 4. Jack, the
Ripper—Influence—Fiction. 5. Large type books. I. Title.
  PR6102.O49N68 2011b
  823'.92—dc22                                                              2011028133

Published in 2011 by arrangement with St. Martin's Press, LLC.

Printed in the United States of America
1 2 3 4 5 6 7 15 14 13 12 11

For Andrew, who reads my books first;
and for Hal, who can't wait to get
started.

BLIND-MAN'S-BUFF.

*(As played by the Police.)*

"TURN ROUND THREE TIMES,
AND CATCH WHOM YOU MAY!"

# PROLOGUE

*Eleven years ago*
Leaves, mud and grass deaden sound. Even screams. The girl knows this. Any sound she might make can't possibly travel the quarter-mile to the car headlights and streetlamps, to the illuminated windows of tall buildings that she can see beyond the wall. The nearby city isn't going to help her and screaming will just burn up energy she can't spare.

She's alone. A moment ago she wasn't.

'Cathy,' she says. 'Cathy, this isn't funny.'

Difficult to imagine anything less funny. So why is someone giggling? Then another sound. A grinding, scraping noise.

She could run. The bridge isn't far. She might make it.

If she runs, she leaves Cathy behind.

A breeze stirs the leaves of the tree she's standing beside and she finds she can't stop shaking. She dressed, a few hours ago, for a hot pub and a heated bus-ride home, not this open space at midnight. Knowing that any second now she may have to run, she lifts first one foot and then the other and takes off her shoes.

'I've had enough now,' she says, in a voice that doesn't sound like her own. She steps forward, away from the tree, a little closer to the great slab of rock lying ahead of her on the grass. 'Cathy,' she says, 'where are you?'

Only the scraping answers back.

The stones look taller at night. Not just bigger, but blacker and older. Yet the circle they make seems to have shrunk. She has a sense of those just out of her line of sight slipping closer, playing grandmother's footsteps; that if she spins round now, there they'll be, close enough to touch.

Unthinkable not to turn with an idea like that in her head; not to whimper when a dark shape plainly is moving closer. One of the tall stones has split in two like a splinter of rock breaking away from a cliff. The splinter stands free and steps forward.

She runs then, but not for long. Another black shape is blocking her path, cutting off her route to the bridge. She turns. Another. And another. Dark figures make their way towards her. Impossible to run. Useless to scream. All she can do is turn on the spot, like a rat caught in a trap. They take hold of her and drag her towards the great, flat rock and one thing, at least, becomes clear.

The sound she can hear is that of a blade being sharpened against stone.

■ ■ ■ ■

# PART ONE:
# POLLY

■ ■ ■ ■

'The brutality of the murder is beyond conception and beyond description.'

*Star,* 31 August 1888

# 1

*Friday 31 August*

A dead woman was leaning against my car.

Somehow managing to stand upright, arms outstretched, fingers grasping the rim of the passenger door, a dead woman was spewing blood over the car's paintwork, each spatter overlaying the last as the pattern began to resemble a spider's web.

A second later she turned and her eyes met mine. Dead eyes. A savage wound across her throat gaped open; her abdomen was a mass of scarlet. She reached out; I couldn't move. She was clutching me, strong for a dead woman.

I know, I know, she was on her feet, still moving, but it was impossible to look into those eyes and think of her as anything other than dead. Technically, the body might be clinging on, the weakening heart still beating, she had a little control over her muscles. Technicalities, all of them. Those eyes knew the game was up.

Suddenly I was hot. Before the sun went down, it had been a warm evening, the sort when London's buildings and pavements cling to the heat of the day, hitting you with a wave of hot air when you venture outside. This was something new, though, this pumping, sticky warmth. This heat had nothing to do with the weather.

I hadn't seen the knife. But I could feel the handle of it now, pressing against me. She was holding me so tightly, was pushing the blade further into her own body.

*No, don't do that.*

I tried to hold her away, just enough to take the pressure off the knife. She coughed, except the cough came from the wound on her throat, not her mouth. Something splashed over my face and then the world turned around us.

We'd fallen. She sank to the ground and I went with her, hitting the tarmac hard and jarring my shoulder. Now she was lying flat on the pavement, staring up at the sky, and I was kneeling over her. Her chest was still moving — just.

There's still time, I told myself, knowing there wasn't. I needed help. None to be had. The small car park was deserted. Tall build-ings of six- and eight-storey blocks of flats

16

surrounded us and, for a second, I caught a movement on one of the balconies. Then nothing. The twilight was deepening by the second.

She'd been attacked moments ago. Whoever had done it would be close.

I was reaching for my radio, patting pockets, not finding it, and all the while watching the woman's eyes. My bag had fallen a few feet away. I fumbled inside and found my mobile, summoning police and ambulance to the car park outside Victoria House on the Brendon Estate in Kennington. When I ended the call, I realized she'd taken hold of my hand.

A dead woman was holding my hand, and it was almost beyond me to look into those eyes and see them trying to focus on mine. I had to talk to her, keep her conscious. I couldn't listen to the voice in my head telling me it was over.

'It's OK,' I was saying. 'It's OK.'

The situation was clearly a very long way from OK.

'Help's coming,' I said, knowing she was beyond help. 'Everything's going to be fine.'

We lie to dying people, I realized that evening, just as the first sirens sounded in the distance.

'Can you hear them? People are coming.

Just hold on.' Both her hand and mine were sticky with blood. The metal strap of her watch pressed into me. 'Come on, stay with me.' Sirens getting louder. 'Can you hear them? They're almost here.'

Footsteps running. I looked up to see flashing blue lights reflected in several windows. A patrol car had pulled up next to my Golf and a uniformed constable was jogging towards us, speaking into his radio. He reached us and crouched down.

'Hold on now,' I said. 'People are here, we'll take care of you.'

The constable had a hand on my shoulder. 'Take it easy,' he was saying, just as I'd done seconds earlier, only he was saying it to me. 'There's an ambulance on its way. Just take it easy.'

The officer was in his mid forties, heavy set, with thinning grey hair. I thought perhaps I'd seen him before.

'Can you tell me where you're hurt?' he asked.

I turned back to the dead woman. Really dead now.

'Love, can you talk to me? Can you tell me your name? Tell me where you're injured?'

No doubt about it. Pale-blue eyes fixed. Body motionless. I wondered if she'd heard

18

anything I'd said to her. She had the most beautiful hair, I noticed then, the palest shade of ash blonde. It spread out around her head like a fan. Her earrings were reflecting light from the streetlamps and there was something about the way they sparkled through strands of her hair that struck me as familiar. I released her hand and began pushing myself up from the pavement. Gently, someone kept me where I was.

'I don't think you should move, love. Wait till the ambulance gets here.'

I hadn't the heart to argue, so I just kept staring at the dead woman. Blood had spattered across the lower part of her face. Her throat and chest were awash with it. It was pooling beneath her on the pavement, finding tiny nicks in the paving stones to travel along. In the middle of her chest, I could just make out the fabric of her shirt. Lower down her body, it was impossible. The wound on her throat wasn't the worst of her injuries, not by any means. I remembered hearing once that the average female body contained around five litres of blood. I'd just never considered quite what it would look like when it was all spilling out.

# 2

'I'm ok, I'm not hurt. It's not my blood.'

I wanted to stand up; they wouldn't let me move.

Three paramedics were huddled around the blonde woman. They seemed to be holding pressure pads against the wound on her abdomen. I heard mention of a tracheotomy. Then something about a peripheral pulse.

*Shall we call it? I think so, she's gone.*

They were turning to me now. I got to my feet. The woman's blood was sticky against my skin, already drying in the warm air. I felt myself sway and saw movement. The blocks of flats surrounding the square had long balconies running the length of every floor. A few minutes ago they'd been deserted. Now they were packed with people. From the back pocket of my jeans I pulled out my warrant card and held it up to the nearest officer.

'DC Lacey Flint,' I said.

He read it and looked into my eyes for confirmation. 'Thought you looked familiar,' he said. 'Based at Southwark, are you?'

I nodded.

'CID,' he said to the hovering paramedics who, having realized there was nothing they could do for the blonde woman, had turned their attention on me. One of them moved forward. I stepped back.

'You shouldn't touch me,' I said. 'I'm not hurt.' I looked down at my bloodstained clothes, feeling dozens of eyes staring at me. 'I'm evidence.'

I wasn't allowed to slink off quietly to the anonymity of the nearest police station. DC Stenning, the first detective on the scene, had received a call from the DI in charge. She was on her way and didn't want me going anywhere until she'd had chance to speak to me.

Pete Stenning had been a colleague of mine at Southwark before he'd joined the area's Major Investigation Team, or MIT, based at Lewisham. He wasn't much older than me, maybe around thirty, and was one of those lucky types blessed with almost universal popularity. Men liked him because he worked hard, but not so hard anyone

21

around felt threatened, he liked down-to-earth, working-class sports like football but could hold down a conversation about golf or cricket, he didn't talk over-much but whatever he said was sensible. Women liked him because he was tall and slim, with curly dark hair and a cheeky grin.

He nodded in my direction, but was too busy trying to keep the public back to come over. By this time, screens has been erected around the blonde woman's body. Deprived of the more exciting sight, everyone wanted to look at me. News had spread. People had sent text messages to friends, who'd hot-footed it over to join in the fun. I sat in the back of a patrol car, avoiding prying eyes and trying to do my job.

The first sixty minutes after a major incident are the most important, when evidence is fresh and the trail to the perpetrator still hot. There are strict protocols we have to follow. I didn't work on a murder team, my day-to-day job involved tracing owners of stolen property and was far less exciting, but I knew I had to remember as much as possible. I was good at detail, a fact I wasn't always grateful for when the dull jobs invariably came my way, but I should be glad of it now.

'Got you a cup of tea, love.' The PC who'd

appointed himself my minder was back. 'You might want to drink it quick,' he added, handing it over. 'The DI's arrived.'

I followed his glance and saw that a silver Mercedes sports car had pulled up not far from my own car. Two people got out. The man was tall and even at a distance I could see he was no stranger to the gym. He was wearing jeans and a grey polo shirt. Tanned arms. Sunglasses.

The woman I recognized immediately from photographs. Slim as a model, with shiny, dark hair cut into a chin-length bob, she was wearing the sort of jeans women pay over a hundred pounds for. She was the newest senior recruit to the twenty-seven major investigation teams based around London and her arrival had been covered officially, in internal circulars, and unofficially on the various police blog sites. She was young for the role of DI, not much more than mid thirties, but she'd just worked a high-profile case in Scotland. She was also rumoured to know more about HOLMES 2, the major incident computer system, than practically any other serving UK police officer. Of course, it didn't hurt, one or two of the less supportive blogs had remarked, that she was female and not entirely white.

I watched her and the man pull on pale-blue Tyvek suits and shoe covers. She tucked her hair into the hood. Then they went behind the screens, the man standing aside at the last moment to allow her to go first.

By this time, white-suited figures were making their way around the site like phantoms. The scene-of-crime officers had arrived. They would establish an inner cordon around the body and an outer one around the crime scene. From now on, everyone entering the cordons would be signed in and out, the exact time of their arrival and departure being recorded. I'd learned all this at the crime academy, only a few months ago, but it was the first time I'd seen it in practice.

A gazebo-like structure was being erected over the spot where the corpse still lay. Screens has already been put up to create walls and within seconds the investigators had a large, enclosed area in which to work. Police tape was set up around my car. Lights were being unloaded from the van just as the DI and her companion emerged. They spoke together for a few seconds then the man turned and walked off, striding over the striped tape that marked the edge of the cordon. The DI came my way.

'I'll leave you to it,' said my minder. I handed him my cup and he moved away. The new DI was standing in front of me. Even in the Tyvek suit she looked elegant. Her skin was a rich, dark cream and her eyes green. I remembered reading that her mother had been Indian.

'DC Flint?' she asked, in a soft Scottish accent. I nodded.

'We haven't met,' she went on. 'I'm Dana Tulloch.'

# 3

'Ok,' said DI Tulloch. 'Go slowly and keep talking.'

I set off, my feet rustling on the pavement. Tulloch had taken one look at me and insisted that a Tyvek suit and slippers be brought. I'd be getting cold, she said, in spite of the warm evening, and I'd attract much less attention if the bloodstains were covered up. I was also wearing a pair of latex gloves to preserve any evidence on my hands.

'I'd been on the third floor,' I said. 'Flat 37. I came down that flight of stairs and turned right.'

'What were you doing there?'

'Talking to a witness.' I stopped and corrected myself. 'A potential witness,' I went on. 'I've been coming over on Friday evenings for a few weeks now. It's the one time I can be pretty certain not to see her mother. I'm trying to persuade her to testify in a case and her mother isn't keen.'

'Did you succeed?' asked Tulloch.

I shook my head. 'No,' I admitted.

We reached the end of the walkway and could see the square again. Uniform were trying to persuade people to go home and not having much luck.

'Guess there isn't much on TV tonight,' muttered Tulloch. 'Which case?'

'Gang rape,' I replied, knowing I could probably expect trouble. I didn't work on crime involving sexual assault and earlier that evening I'd been moonlighting. A few years ago the Met set up a number of bespoke teams known as the Sapphire Units to deal with all such offences. It was the sort of work I'd joined the police service to do and I was waiting for a vacancy to come up. In the meantime, I kept up to speed on what was going on. I couldn't help myself.

'Was the passage empty when you came out of the stairwell?' Tulloch asked.

'I think so,' I said, although the truth was I wasn't sure. I'd been annoyed at the response I'd got from Rona, my potential witness; I'd been thinking about my next move, if I even had one. I hadn't been paying much attention to what was going on around me.

'When you came out into the square, what

did you see? How many people?'

Slowly, we retraced the last time I'd walked this way, with Tulloch firing questions at me every few seconds. Annoyed with myself for not being more alert earlier, I tried my best. I didn't think there'd been anyone around. There'd been music, some sort of loud rap that I hadn't recognized. A helicopter had passed overhead, lower than normal, because I'd glanced up at it. I was certain I'd never seen the blonde woman before tonight. There had been something, for a second, as I'd looked at her, something niggling, but no, it had gone.

'I was looking back at this point,' I said, as I turned on the spot. 'There was a loud noise behind me.'

I met Tulloch's eye and knew what she was thinking. I'd looked back and had probably missed seeing the attack by seconds. Split seconds.

'When did you see her?' she asked me.

'I was a bit closer,' I replied. 'I was fumbling in my bag as I was walking — I thought I might have left my car keys behind — then I looked up and saw her.'

We were right back in the thick of it. A white-suited figure was taking photographs of the blood spatter on my car.

'Go on,' she told me.

'I didn't see the blood at first,' I said. 'I thought she'd stopped to ask directions, that maybe she thought there was someone in the car.'

'Tell me what she looked like. Describe her to me.'

'Tall,' I began, not sure where this was going. She'd just seen the woman in question for herself.

She sighed. 'You're a detective, Flint. How tall?'

'Five ten,' I guessed. 'Taller than both of us. And slim.'

Her eyebrows went up.

'Size twelve,' I said quickly. 'From the back I thought she was young, probably because she was slim and well dressed, but when I saw her face, she seemed older than I expected.'

'Go on.'

'She looked good,' I went on, warming to my theme. If Tulloch wanted endless detail I could oblige. 'She was well dressed. Her clothes looked expensive. Simple, but well made. Her hair had been professionally done. That colour doesn't come out of a bottle you buy at Boots and there was no sign of roots. Her skin was good and so were her teeth, but she had lines around her eyes and her jawline wasn't that tight.'

'So you'd put her age at . . .'

'I'd say well-preserved mid forties.'

'Yes, so would I.' There was movement all around us, but Tulloch's eyes weren't leaving my face. There could have been just the two of us in the car park.

'Did she have ID?' I asked. 'Do we know who she is?'

'Nothing in her bag,' said a man's voice. I turned. Tulloch's companion of earlier had joined us. He'd pushed his sunglasses on to the top of his head. There was scarring around his right eye that looked recent. 'No ID, no car keys, some cash and bits of make-up,' he went on. 'Mystery how she got here. We're some distance from the Tube and she doesn't strike me as a bus type.'

Tulloch was looking at the large blocks of flats that surrounded the square.

'Course, her car keys could have been stolen along with the car. A woman like that probably drives a nice motor,' he said. He had a faint south London accent.

'She had diamond studs in her ears,' I said. 'This wasn't a robbery.'

He looked at me. His eyes were blue, almost turquoise. The one with the scarring around it was bloodshot. 'Could have been fake,' he suggested.

'If I was slitting someone's throat and cutting open their stomach to rob them, I'd take any visible jewellery on the off-chance, wouldn't you?' I said. 'And she had a nice-looking wristwatch too. I could feel it scratching against my hand as she died.'

He didn't like that, I could tell. He raised his hand to rub his sore eye and frowned at me.

'Flint, this is DI Joesbury,' said Tulloch. 'Nothing to do with the investigation. He only came out with me tonight because he's bored. This is DC Flint. Lacey, I think, is that right?'

'Which reminds me,' said Joesbury, who'd barely acknowledged the introduction. 'Lewisham want to know when you're bringing her in.'

Tulloch was still looking at the buildings around us. 'I don't get it, Mark,' she said. 'We're surrounded by flats and it isn't that late, dozens of people could have witnessed what happened. Why would you murder someone here?'

From somewhere nearby I could hear a dog barking.

'Well, she wasn't here by chance,' replied Joesbury. 'That woman belongs in Knights-bridge, not Kennington. Thanks to DC Flint's knowledge of jewellery, we know that robbery seems unlikely, although we do

31

need to find her car.'

'Kids round here wouldn't kill for a car,' I said as they both turned to me. 'Oh, they'd steal it, no question, but they'd just snatch the keys, give her a shove. They wouldn't need to —'

'Slash her throat so deeply they cut right through her windpipe?' finished Joesbury. 'Cut her abdomen from the breastbone down to the pubic bone. No, you're right, DC Flint, that does seem like overkill.'

OK, I was definitely not getting good vibes from this bloke. I took a step back, then another. For some reason, probably shock, I'd talked much more than I would normally. Maybe I just needed to quieten down for a while. Keep a low profile.

'How?' said Tulloch.

'Sorry?' said Joesbury, who'd been watching me back away.

'She was still on her feet when DC Flint saw her,' said Tulloch. 'Still alive, although horribly injured. That means she was attacked seconds before. Probably even while Flint was wandering around fumbling in her bag for her keys. How did he do it? How did he inflict those injuries then disappear completely?'

Wandering and fumbling? Tulloch had made the attack sound like it was my fault.

32

I almost opened my mouth again and remembered just in time. Low profile.

'There are no CCTV cameras in the square,' said Joesbury. 'But the high street is just yards away. Stenning has gone to round up any footage. If our villain left the estate, he'll have been picked up on one of them.'

Maybe it had been my fault. If I'd had my wits about me, I might have seen the attacker before he struck. I could have yelled for help, summoned local uniform on my radio. I could have stopped the attack. Shit, that sort of guilt trip was all I needed.

'Whoever did it would be covered in blood,' said Joesbury, still looking at me. 'They'll have left a trail.' He glanced behind. 'Sounds like the dogs are here.'

We looked towards the car park. Two dogs had arrived. German Shepherds, each with its own handler.

'Not necessarily,' I said, before I could stop myself. They both turned back to me. 'If her throat was cut from behind, whoever did it might have escaped being splashed. All her blood spattered forward. On to my car.'

'And then on to you,' said Joesbury, his eyes dropping away from my face to the bloodstains that were just about visibl through the Tyvek. 'Are we done her

Tully?' he went on. 'You really need to get DC Flint back to the station.'

Tulloch looked uncertain for a moment. 'I just need to make sure Neil —'

'Anderson knows exactly what he's doing,' said Joesbury. 'He's got six officers taking witness statements, the traffic has been redirected and they'll start the door-to-door as soon as the dogs are done.'

'Can you take her back?' asked Tulloch. 'I want to have a good look round when things quieten down.'

Joesbury looked as though he were about to argue, then smiled at her. He had very good teeth. 'Do I get to drive the Tullymobile?' he asked.

Shaking her head, Tulloch pulled down the zip of her pale-blue suit and dug into her pocket. Glaring, she handed over her car keys. 'Prang it and I prang you,' she warned.

'Come on, Flint, before she changes her mind.' Joesbury had put a hand on my elbow and was steering me towards the DI's silver Mercedes.

'And make sure she keeps that suit on,' called Tulloch, as Joesbury held the passenger door open and I climbed inside. The interior looked showroom new. I sank back against the leather seat and closed my eyes.

# 4

It was gone nine o'clock by this time, but the streets were still busy and we didn't make great progress. I was still smarting from Tulloch's comments about wandering and fumbling, so I kept my eyes closed and asked myself what I could have done differently. Joesbury said nothing.

After ten, maybe fifteen minutes of silence, he switched on the car stereo and the eerie notes of Clannad filled the car.

'Oh, you are kidding me,' he muttered under his breath. 'Is there anything in the glove compartment?'

I opened my eyes and, still wearing latex gloves, pulled out the only CD in the small compartment. 'Medieval plainsong,' I said, reading the cover.

Joesbury shook his head. 'If you get chance to speak to her about her taste in music, go for it,' he said. 'She had me listening to Westlife the other night.'

He lapsed into silence again as we reached the Old Kent Road. Occasionally, as the streetlights caught the car windscreen at the right angle, I could see his reflection. Nothing out of the ordinary. Late thirties, I guessed, brown hair cut short. He hadn't shaved for a couple of days. His face and bare forearms were suntanned. His teeth, I'd already noticed, were even and very white.

Another ten minutes passed without either of us speaking. I had a sense, though, partly from the way his head kept tilting, that he was watching me in the car windscreen too.

*Wandering and fumbling.*

'If I'd got to her sooner, would she have lived?' I asked, as we turned off Lewisham High Street and into the car park behind the station.

'Guess we'll never know,' replied Joesbury. There were no spaces left so he parked directly behind a green Audi, completely blocking it in.

'She was still alive seconds before the ambulance arrived,' I said. 'I should have put something against the wound, shouldn't I? Tried to stop the bleeding.'

If I was hoping for any sort of comfort from this guy, I was wasting my breath. 'I'm a police officer, not a paramedic,' he replied, switching off the engine. 'Looks like you're expected.'

The station's duty sergeant, a scene-of-crime officer and a police doctor were waiting for us. Together we walked through the barred rear door of Lewisham police station and my arrival was officially recorded. I'd worked for the Metropolitan Police for nearly four years, but had a feeling I was about to see it from a very different perspective.

Some time later, I sat staring at dirty cream walls and grey floor tiles. My left shoulder was sore from where I'd fallen on it earlier and I could feel a headache threatening. Over the past hour, I'd been asked to undress completely before being examined by a police doctor. After a shower, I'd been examined again, and photographed. My fingernails had been clipped, my saliva swabbed and my hair combed thoroughly and painfully. Then I'd been given a pair of orange overalls normally issued to prisoners in custody.

I hadn't eaten that evening and, whether it was due to low blood sugar, shock or just a cold room, I was finding it hard to stop shivering. I kept seeing pale-blue eyes, staring at me.

I could have saved her. If I hadn't been in my own little world, we might not be kicking off a murder investigation right now. And everyone knew that. It would be my legacy, for as long as I stayed in the service: the DC who'd let a woman be stabbed to death right in front of her.

The door opened and DI Joesbury came in. In the small room he seemed taller than he had on the street or even in DI Tulloch's car. DC Gayle Mizon, the detective who'd assisted the police doctor in examining me, was with him. The two of them had been laughing at something in the corridor outside and he was still smiling as he held the door open for her. He had a great smile. Then he turned to me and the smile faded.

'Still bored?' I asked, before I could stop myself.

I might not have spoken. I got no reaction whatsoever.

Mizon was an attractive blonde woman of around thirty-three or -four. She'd brought me coffee. I put my hand on the mug for warmth but didn't dare pick it up. I was shaking too much. Joesbury continued to study me, my hair still wet from the shower, my face dry and pink because it hadn't been moisturized, and my prisoner-in-custody uniform. He didn't look impressed.

'Right,' he said. 'Let's take a statement.'

By the time he called a halt, I'd barely the energy left to sit upright in my chair. If I'd wanted to be tactful about DI Joesbury's interviewing technique, I'd have said he was thorough. If honesty had been the order of the day, I'd have called him a sadistic shit.

Before we started, they explained that Gayle Mizon would be taking the statement, Joesbury only sitting in on an advisory capacity. They'd even given me chance to request he leave the room. I'd shrugged and muttered something about it being fine. Big mistake, because the moment the interview kicked off, he took charge.

What followed didn't feel like any witness statement I'd ever been a party to before. More like I was about to be charged. He made me go over every detail several times, until even Mizon was looking uncomfortable. And he kept going back to the same point. How could I not have seen something? How could I have missed the attack and yet been close enough for her to die in my arms? Every second I was waiting for him to say that the blonde woman would still be alive if I hadn't messed up.

Finally, he terminated the interview and switched off the recording equipment. The clock on the wall said ten past eleven.

'Is there someone you'd like us to call?' asked Mizon, as Joesbury took the disc out of the recording machine and labelled it.

I shook my head.

'Will there be someone at home when you get there?' she asked me. 'Flatmate? Boyfriend? You've had a nasty shock. You probably shouldn't be on your own.'

'I live on my own,' I said. 'But I'm fine,' I added, when she looked concerned. 'Is it OK if I go now?'

'Family?' Mizon wasn't giving up easily.

'They don't live in London,' I said, which was true, if a bit disingenuous. They don't live anywhere. I have no family. 'Look, I'm tired, I haven't eaten, I just want to get home and —'

Joesbury looked up, frowning. 'Did nobody offer you food?' he asked, and really, you had to admire the way he made it sound like it was my own fault.

'Really not a problem. Can I go now?' I stood up. 'Sir,' I added, for good measure.

Joesbury turned to Mizon. 'Gayle, if we'd brought the killer in red-handed, knife dangling from his teeth, we'd have fed him. One of our own, we leave to starve.'

'I thought someone else was . . .' Mizon began.

'It's really not . . .' I tried.

'Sorry,' she said to me. I shrugged, managed a smile.

Joesbury stood up and crossed the room. 'Come on,' he said, holding the door open.

'Where are we going now?' I hadn't the energy to even try being polite any more. Not that previous efforts had been all that successful.

'I'm getting you fed, then I'm getting you home,' he replied. He nodded at the disc on the table. 'Can you get that processed?' he said to a rather surprised-looking Mizon. Then he walked me out of the station.

Tulloch's silver Mercedes had already been moved and Joesbury opened up the green Audi we'd blocked in previously. He turned on the engine, put the car into gear and began flicking through a stack of CDs.

'Got any Westlife?' I asked, as he reversed the car out of the parking space and turned it round. When he didn't reply, I made a mental note that a sense of humour wasn't high on this guy's list of attributes. And that I could probably cross out fair-minded and compassionate as well. In fact, so far, the only box I could tick was a healthy respect for a woman's need to eat. He pushed a CD into the stereo. Back on Lewisham High Street, he turned the volume right up and

41

rhythmic, percussion-based club music filled the car. Message received and understood, DI Joesbury, I wasn't meant to talk.

# 5

The garden is long and narrow. And very dark. Whilst high walls on three sides keep out most of the streetlight, the dense foliage of over-mature shrubs seems to soak up any light that does seep through. The garden is overlooked by several windows, but the intruder moving slowly down the slim gravel path is dressed entirely in black and is unlikely to be seen.

The garden is scented. The intruder stops for a moment and takes a deep breath, before stretching out a hand to a tiny, star-shaped flower. Jasmine.

At the bottom of the garden is a small, neat wooden shed, partially hidden by vegetation. Ivy creeps up its walls and overhanging tree branches rest on its roof. The door is locked, but the intruder thinks for a moment before reaching up to run a hand along the rim of the low, flat roof. After a few seconds the hand finds what it is looking for. A key.

The door opens easily. The intruder starts back with a muttered curse.

For a moment, a human form appears to be hanging in the shed. It swings gently, turning on the spot. Human in form, but not human. This has a soft, cylindrical torso, it wears clothes but is limbless. Its head — male — once stared out from a shop window.

The intruder touches it lightly. It spins on the chain that suspends it from the shed roof and the head lolls like that of a drunk. Or a crazy man.

'What a good idea,' says the intruder. 'Oh Lacey, what a brilliantly good idea.'

# 6

'Are you veggie, lactose intolerant, allergic to sesame seeds . . . ?' Joesbury was asking me, practically the first words to come out of his mouth since we'd left the station. We were in a small Chinese restaurant, not far from where I live, that I didn't think I'd ever noticed before. The owner, a slim Chinese man in his fifties called Trev, had greeted Joesbury like an old friend.

'If it stays still long enough I'll eat it,' I replied.

Joesbury's eyes opened a little wider. He and Trev shared a look, had a short, muttered conversation and then the Chinese man disappeared. Joesbury took the seat opposite mine and I waited with something like interest. He was going to have to talk to me now.

He picked up a fork and ran the prongs down a paper napkin, before leaning back to admire the four perfectly straight lines he'd made. He glanced up, caught my eye and looked down again. The fork made its way down the napkin once more. It was becoming blindingly obvious that DI Joesbury and I weren't of the same mind on the talking issue.

'If you're not part of the MIT, what do you do?' I asked. 'Traffic?'

If you want to insult a fellow cop, you ask him if he works on traffic. Quite why I was insulting a senior officer I'd only just met was, of course, a good question.

'I work for SO10,' he replied.

I thought about it for a second. SO stood for Special Operations. The divisions were numbered according to the particular function they served. SO1 protected public figures, SO14, the royal family. 'SO10 do undercover work, don't they?' I asked.

He inclined his head. 'Covert operations is the term they prefer these days,' he said.

'Then you're based at Scotland Yard?' I asked, slightly encouraged at getting a whole sentence out of him.

Another brief nod. 'Technically,' he said.

Now what did that mean? Either you're based somewhere or you're not.

'So how come you ended up at the scene tonight?'

He sighed, as though wondering why I was

bothering him with this tiresome conversation business. 'I'm convalescing,' he said. 'Dislocated my shoulder and nearly lost an eye in a fight. Officially, I'm on light duties only until November, but as both you and DI Tulloch have been at pains to point out, I'm bored.'

Trev arrived back with drinks. He put a bottle of South American beer down in front of each of us. I hadn't been asked what I wanted.

'The look on your face says you're not a beer drinker,' said Joesbury, reaching across and pouring the contents of my bottle into a glass. 'And the look on mine should tell you, I know that — you're far too skinny to be a beer drinker — but it's good for shock.'

I picked up my glass. I'm not a beer drinker, but alcohol of any description was starting to feel like a very good idea. Joesbury watched me drink nearly a third of its contents before coming up for air.

'What brought you into the police?' he asked me.

'An early fascination with serial killers,' I replied. It was the truth, although I didn't usually advertise the fact in quite so blunt a fashion. I'd been intrigued by violent crime and its perpetrators for as long as I could remember and it was this that had led me, through a long and circuitous path, into the police service.

Joesbury raised one eyebrow at me.

'Sadistic, psychopathic predators specifically,' I went on. 'You know, the type who kill to satisfy some deviant sexual longing. Sutcliffe, West, Brady. When I was a kid I couldn't get enough of them.'

The eyebrow stayed up as I realized my glass was now more than half empty and that I really needed to slow down a bit.

'You know, if you're bored, you should think about golf,' I said. 'A lot of middle-aged men find it fills the hours quite nicely.'

Joesbury's lips tightened, but he wasn't about to dignify such a cheap jibe with a response. And I really had to get a grip. Winding up a senior officer, however unpleasant, just wasn't me. I was low-profile girl.

'Sir, I apologize,' I said. 'I've had one hell of an evening and —' Movement at my side. The food had arrived.

'Don't call him Sir,' said Trev, putting a plate of noodles with prawns and vegetables in front of me and something with beef and black beans in Joesbury's place. 'Young female officers calling him Sir turns him on something rotten.'

'I'll remember that,' I muttered, thinking

it probably shouldn't be too hard. Joesbury was definitely not my type. I didn't actually have a type. But if I had, he wouldn't be it.

'Now this is for Dana,' Trev went on, putting a covered plastic dish on the table. 'Give her my love, tell her to come and see me soon, and if she ever gets tired —'

'Trev,' drawled Joesbury. 'How many times . . . ?'

'A man can dream,' said Trev, as he made his way back to the kitchen. When I looked up, Joesbury was intent on his food.

'How did he know I'm police?' I asked, picking up my fork and pushing a prawn around in a circle.

'You're wearing an orange Andy Pandy suit with PROPERTY OF THE METROPOLITAN POLICE on the collar,' said Joesbury, without looking up.

'I could be a villain,' I said, putting the prawn in my mouth. It sat there, large and uncomfortably dry, on my tongue.

'Yeah,' said Joesbury, putting his fork down and lifting his eyes. 'The thought had crossed my mind.'

# 7

I live just off the Wandsworth Road, less than five minutes' walk from Trev's Chinese restaurant, in part of an old Victorian house. The letting agent who rented it to me called it the garden flat. In truth, it was the basement, accessible via a dozen stone steps that led down from the pavement, just to the right of the house's front door. Out of habit, I checked the small area of shadow in the under-well of the steps. If I was unlucky (and careless) one night, someone could be waiting. It had never happened yet and I rather hoped tonight wouldn't be the first time; I was hardly in the mood. The stairwell was empty and the padlock on the door of the shed where I keep my bike hadn't been disturbed. I slipped my key into the lock and went inside.

I walked through my living room, past the tiny galley kitchen and into my bedroom. I'd changed the sheets that morning, as I always do on Friday. They were crisp white cotton, one of the very few luxuries I allow myself. Normally, getting into bed on a Friday night is one of the highlights of my week.

But I had just the worst feeling that if I lay down on them, when I got up again, they'd be stained the dark red of another woman's blood. Stupid, I'd showered until my skin felt raw, but . . .

I carried on walking, through a sort of lean-to conservatory and into the garden. It's long and very narrow, like lots of gardens behind London's terraced streets, attracting practically no direct sunlight. Luckily, though, whoever designed it knew what they were doing. All the plants thrive in the shade and it's full of small trees and dense shrubs. High brick walls on either side give me privacy. There's a side door that leads to an alley. I keep it locked.

I closed my eyes, and saw pale-blue ones staring into mine. Oh no.

DI Joesbury, objectionable git that he was, had actually taken my mind off the events of earlier. Being with him, trying to find something to talk about, trying even harder not to say anything inappropriate, had given me something to focus on. Now, on my own, it was all coming back.

51

London is never quiet, and even at this hour I could hear the constant hum of traffic, the sound of people walking past in the street and high-pitched yelling from very nearby.

There is a park not a hundred metres from my flat. When the sun goes down the teenagers of south London claim it for their own, swinging around the play equipment like monkeys, screeching and howling at each other. They were on form tonight. From what I could hear there was some sort of chase going on. Girls were squealing. Music playing. They were letting off some steam.

Which, exhausted or not, was exactly what I needed to do. And I had a playground of my own I could go to.

# 8

Camden town has long been one of the trendiest places in north London and especially so since the development of the Camden Stables Market. Once an extensive network of tunnels, arches, viaducts and passageways, the area was sold off to developers some years ago and transformed into a vast complex of shops, bars, market stalls and cafés. It's popular in the daytime as a place to browse, eat and just hang out. At night, people flock here. At least once a week, usually on a Friday, I'm one of them.

My car had been taken away by the scene-of-crime officers so I'd had to travel by bus. As I approached the Horse Hospital, once stabling for sick or tired horses that worked on the railways, I took off my jacket and tucked it into the small rucksack I was carrying over one shoulder.

Horses, or rather their replicas, are the predominant feature of the Stables Market.

Back in the days of the railway's construction, hundreds of them were kept to transport goods and equipment to, from and around the site. Nothing so unusual in that, but in Camden the working horses led a largely subterranean life, moving from one area to another through tunnels, built specifically to allow them a safe and convenient passage around. At one time they were even stabled underground.

These days, the living, working beasts are long gone, but equine images are everywhere you turn. There are wall hangings, massive free-standing statues, motifs built into railings, on lamp posts, even on bins. I like horses, but even I'm inclined to feel the developers have overdone it a bit.

The heat hit me like a wall when I stepped through the main door of the Horse Hospital. Violet lights twinkled on either side as I made my way through the central passageway, past the original layout of loose boxes and stable furniture. Even at this hour the place was full and the air was thick with the smell of alcohol and humanity.

A party was going on in one of the boxes and for a second I considered gate-crashing. Then I noticed red helium balloons around the iron grilles. They swayed, gleaming, in the hot air. Like blood droplets. I carried on, pushed my way to the bar and bought a Bombay Sapphire on ice. I can't bear the taste so I drink it very slowly, but if I need a quick shot, it does the job. The clock behind the bar told me it was five to one in the morning. The place closed at two.

A few more paces and I was surrounded by the soft tangerine light of the photographic gallery. Around me golden faces glistened with heat. A band had been playing earlier and up on the stage someone was packing away sound equipment.

'Hey baby!' Four boys, barely old enough to drink, were blocking my way. The one who'd spoken staggered closer, put a hand out towards me.

'Want to step outside?' he offered.

The hand had made contact with my hip. He was having trouble focusing and I didn't think it was just the booze.

'Well, it's a sweet thought,' I said, 'but I haven't had the all-clear from the clinic yet. I'll get back to you.'

I smiled quickly at a tall, dark-haired boy who seemed more sober than the rest. He grinned back and I stepped past them. Before I'd gone more than a few feet I felt a hand on my arm. The dark-haired boy had followed me.

'Don't rush off,' he said.

I looked at him and thought about it. Younger than I preferred, but otherwise definitely possible. Tall, just starting to fill out. He had a strong jawline and his face an almost regal look about it. His hair was curly, a few inches long, and he had pale skin. The sort that was very soft.

'What's your name?' I said.

'Ben,' he replied. 'Yours?'

Three pairs of eyes were watching us, willing him on. Scratch a gang of mates and you get a gang. I didn't like gangs.

'Catch you another time,' I said. 'Come without your friends.'

I turned away, moved back through the Horse Hospital's loose boxes and stepped outside. A wide, curved walkway known as the horse creep takes you down, past another giant equine statue, to the market below. The night was cooling down. Most of the outdoor stalls had closed up for the night, but those serving food were still doing business. Everywhere I looked, people were huddled in groups, leaning against walls and railings, keeping warm under outdoor heaters, eating, drinking.

At the centre of the piazza, wide steps lead down to more market stalls. The top was as good a vantage point as any. About halfway down, a fair-haired man was watching me.

As I stared back he didn't look away. When I smiled, he smiled too.

He seemed to be alone, leaning against one of the metal horse statues. Around thirty, I guessed, maybe a bit older, still in a business suit. He'd removed his tie and unbuttoned the top of his shirt. If he'd come straight from work he'd been here a long time, but, even at this distance, I didn't think he was drunk.

As I set off down the stairs he realized I was heading his way. He'd straightened up and was running a finger around his collar. His eyes hadn't left mine and I didn't think he was going to be one of my more difficult conquests. Then something made me look up and I stopped dead.

Mark Joesbury was directly opposite me, on the balcony that ran round the steps. He was leaning forward against the railing, his eyes going from me to the man I was heading towards. As he realized I'd seen him, his eyes narrowed.

I carried on walking, blanking the fair-haired man. At the bottom of the steps, I went left and shoved my way through the crowds, pushing a leather-clad girl out of the way, squeezing through bodies. I just had to hope Joesbury didn't know Camden as well as I did.

The crowd was thinning out but getting less respectable as I walked quickly past the toilets. This was where drug deals went down. I pushed through the swing door and started to run up concrete steps. I had to go up several flights to get back to street level.

If Joesbury didn't know about this way out, I could skirt my way around the market stalls, cut through Camden Lock Place and get across the roving bridge. On the other side, I could jog a few hundred yards and get a night bus home. I had flat shoes in my bag.

As I made my way towards the lock, I was shivering again and honestly couldn't have said this time whether it was cold, delayed shock or just plain fury. By the time I'd reached the canal, I'd decided.

What the hell was Joesbury doing here? I come to Camden for a reason, damn it. It's the other side of frigging London from where I live and work and the chances of coming across anyone I know are tiny. It could not be coincidence that he was here. He'd dropped me off, hung around outside my flat and followed me here. Why?

It was after two by the time I got home. I walked straight through the flat. There is a tiny shed at the bottom of the garden. I've put foam matting on the floor and hung a large punchbag from the middle of the shed roof. I've humanized it, giving it a head that once belonged to a shop dummy, dressing it in clothes, so that it resembles a human figure. I rarely bother with gloves.

I hit it as hard as I could; so hard my bruised shoulder yelled at me. Ignoring the pain, I hit it again, then again, until I was so weary I lost my balance and fell over. I gave the bag one last kick and wondered whether, just once, I'd get away with screaming my head off. Instead, I closed my eyes.

I can never remember my dreams. Come morning I have no idea what's passed through my head in the dark hours and yet I always know if my dreams have been bad. They must have been very bad that night, because I woke, hardly an hour after falling asleep, to find myself drenched in sweat and hardly able to breathe. I scrabbled backwards until I hit the shed door and found myself, wide awake, in the garden.

Awake or not, it seemed the dream was hovering around. I could see pale-blue eyes, the dead woman's eyes, staring into mine with something like rage. No, that wasn't right, the eyes had been terrified. Except now the terror was mine. And the eyes were getting closer all the time . . .

The chill night air was taking away some of the heat. I was OK, it was just delayed shock. Just a dream, my first for a very long time. I stumbled halfway across the garden and stopped.

Music was coming from close by, possibly the park. But it wasn't the sort of pounding, pulsing sound I was used to hearing here at night. This was a melody, soft and light, drifting across the rooftops. Julie Andrews from *The Sound of Music,* the song she sings to comfort the children scared of the storm. *Raindrops and roses,* it begins. 'My Favourite Things'.

As a child, I'd been enchanted by *The Sound of Music.* I'd loved this particular song and played the game myself, making lists of my favourite things. When life got completely shit (regular occurrence when I was a kid) I'd played the game and made myself feel a little bit better. But it had all been so long ago.

I took a step closer to the house.

The music was still playing, softly, sweetly, and beneath it, on the other side of the garden wall, I could hear scuffling. Quickly, I checked the side door that led to the alley. The bolt was shut. Something moved again, something brushing against the wall. I

60

wouldn't normally describe myself as a timid person but I felt a sudden need to get indoors.

I hurried across the garden and in through the conservatory, checking the locks more carefully than I normally do. Probably just one of those weird coincidences, and yet, as I pulled a spare blanket from the cupboard and curled up on the sofa, I couldn't help wondering why it should be tonight, of all nights, that someone should decide to play 'My Favourite Things'.

I woke to the sound of my phone ringing. It was the duty sergeant at Southwark. I'd left instructions that if a certain person called for me, I was to be found. That person was now waiting at the station. So, day off or not, I was going into work.

# 9

'They was three of them. At first they was three of them. Then more arrive.'

I sat very still on the wooden bench, not wanting to do anything that might distract her. I really wanted to make notes, but she'd refused to let me. She hadn't allowed me to turn on the tiny recorder I'd brought with me either. She wasn't making a statement, she'd said repeatedly, until she was certain I understood. She wasn't even prepared to stay in the station. So we'd gone out, had walked down towards the river, to the place where Shakespeare's Globe had been re-created on the South Bank.

Rona Dawson was fifteen years old, plump, with gleaming skin and braided hair. Eyes like dark chocolate. She was a good-looking black girl like dozens of others from south London. And like dozens of others, she'd been raped by her boyfriend and

62

several of his mates.

Rape crime, particularly rape by gangs of young men and boys, has become a huge problem in south London. Not too long ago, Scotland Yard statistics showed a trebling in the incidence of gang attacks across the city over the past four years. More than a third of the reported victims were under sixteen.

When it comes to rape, of course, reported incidents are the tip of the iceberg.

'When you arrived at the flat, there was just the three of them?' I asked, when she didn't go on. 'One of them was Miles?'

She nodded.

'And Miles had phoned to ask you to come round?'

She nodded again. 'He say come round and watch a DVD. I thought it would be just the two of us.'

'Miles is your friend, boyfriend . . . ?'

She shrugged. 'I suppose,' she said. 'He's just someone I know.'

A little way to our left the Millennium Bridge was already busy, two steady streams of foot traffic flowing gently along it. Visitors from the north bank crossing to view the Globe or visit the Tate Modern; others walking in the opposite direction, heading for St Paul's Cathedral or the shops and galleries further north. On the first day of September, London was still in peak tourist season.

'Had you had sex with him before?' I asked her. 'Before that day?'

She nodded, without taking her eyes off the river.

'What happened when you arrived?'

'I seen these other two. I didn't know them but I seen them around. We started to watch a film but it didn't feel right.'

A passenger boat was heading our way, its bow sending waves across the water. 'In what way didn't it feel right?' I asked her.

'They was looking at each other, not at the film,' she said. 'They wasn't watching the film. I didn't like it and I said I had to go. That I was meeting Bethany.'

'Did you get up to go?'

She nodded. 'Miles wouldn't let me,' she said. 'He said to come into the bedroom. I didn't want to, I said I had to go, but he pushed me in and shut the door. I said I had a stomachache, but he pushed me down on the bed. I thought if I let him get it over with I could go.'

She looked up at me again, eyes hard, daring me to blame her, to say it was her fault, she'd let him, she hadn't even put up a fight.

'I understand,' I said. 'So you had sex?'

She nodded. 'He was doing it and I heard the door open. I saw the other two standing in the doorway.'

'What did you do?'

'I yelled at them to get out. I told Miles to make them get out, but he just put his hand over my mouth and told me to keep quiet. Then he got up and I tried to get up too, but he pushed me back down again and then the other two were on me.'

Rona's hand was beside me on the bench. I gave it a quick pat, but stopped when she looked surprised. The passenger boat arrived and docked at a small river pier. We watched the crew hook ropes over giant cleats and the passengers begin to disembark.

'Did they threaten you?' I asked, when most of the passengers were on dry land.

She gave a little shrug. 'They just kept saying to keep quiet and they'd let me go,' she said. 'To keep quiet and I wouldn't get hurt.'

The boat was loading up new passengers now. Nothing Rona had told me so far was surprising. I'd heard variations of it several times already from other girls. I'd read countless reports. It was all horribly familiar.

'What happened next, Rona?'

'One of them was kneeling on my shoulders. He pulled my bra up round my neck

65

and put his hands on my . . .' She stopped. She was looking down at her body.

'He put his hands on your breasts?' I asked.

She nodded. 'He was holding me, saying they was the biggest he'd ever seen, he kept repeating it, all the time his mate was doing it to me. It was humiliating, you know what I'm saying?'

'I know. Did you ask them to stop?'

She looked down at her hands.

'I understand that you were scared, Rona,' I said. 'I'm sorry I have to ask you all these questions. I know how hard it must be to answer them. Are you able to go on?'

She nodded. 'When the one who was doing it to me had finished, they swapped. Then, same thing again.'

'Where was Miles while this was happening?'

'Sitting in a chair, watching.'

'Did they let you go, when the third one had raped you?'

She looked at me and shook her head. 'No,' she said. 'They didn't let me go. Two more of them arrived.'

# 10

The underground space is vast and dark and smells of decay, like the cathedral of a city whose inhabitants are long since dead. The day outside was bright and clear, close to noon. Down here, the darkness is all consuming and time has become meaningless. The black-clad figure moves slowly and the huge structure amplifies sound like the inside of a great shell. The echo of each footstep seems to dance away into the distance, as though endlessly repeating itself somewhere out of earshot. The chamber feels like a crypt.

'Perfect,' says a voice.

The water, twenty feet below the searching eyes, looks black as moleskin in the light of the torch. It's shining, giving off the peculiar odour of petrol and salt water that always seems to hover around a river when the tide is heading out. Except this water never moves. This water is still as death.

A sudden sound above. Airborne creatures live in here, whether birds or bats or something new entirely, it's impossible to tell. A stone or piece of brickwork falls into the water. The sound, like glass breaking, cuts through the silence so sharply the air seems to shimmer around it for a moment. Then all is still again.

As the figure in black moves on, the smell seems to evolve. Humanity, street drugs and paraffin: echoes, all of them. It's been years since anyone has been down here. Years, probably, since anyone has even remembered it was once a home.

And yet there are traces, as the footsteps move on, of the people this vaulted space once knew. A lantern with a candle stub inside it, a small, upturned calor-gas stove. The people made dens for themselves with boxes, old curtains, even what looks like a hospital screen. They divided up the huge space to give themselves territory, erected walls for privacy, and most of their structures still exist. Along this long, suspended gallery are a dozen or more hiding places.

A discarded sheet of polythene moves in a sudden breeze and it sounds like the rattle of old bones. The polythene marks the way. The figure reaches out and pushes it to one side. Then steps through.

A smaller space. Still cold, damp and dark, but more containable. There is a mattress on the floor, even an old fold-up chair.

'Perfect,' whispers the voice again. Then, softer still, 'Lacey, I'm home.'

# 11

I talked to Rona for more than an hour. When we were tired of watching the river, we got up and wandered down Bankside. At the bridge we turned back again and joined the crowds admiring the black and white, surprisingly tiny, circular theatre. Everything she told me was off the record. She wasn't prepared to press charges, just wanted someone to talk to. She told me how two more boys had arrived, the older one she thought was seventeen, the younger, her age — fifteen. The five boys had stripped her naked and then the two new arrivals had taken turns to rape her. Then they'd forced her to kneel at the foot of the bed and perform fellatio on each of them. It was an act, she told me, known as a lineup. When that was over, the oldest of the boys had turned her face-down on the bed and raped her anally. Only when they saw how much she was bleeding did they let her go.

Just before she half crawled out of the front door, Miles had given her the money for her bus fare home.

We both knew this case was never coming to court. Rona knew other girls who'd suffered in the same way, she knew the form. If she brought charges against the boys, they'd either deny anything had happened or they'd claim she consented. The fact that she already had a sexual relationship with one of the boys and had gone willingly to his flat would be held against her. The boys had used condoms, again implying some level of consent. Even if they were charged, they were young and could well be released on bail and be back in the neighbourhood. They would have friends, who would be only too happy to intimidate potential witnesses. If Rona went public, she wouldn't be safe.

When she'd finished, it would have been difficult to say which of the two of us was the more exhausted.

'What can I do for you, Rona?' I asked. 'I understand that you don't feel able to press charges right now, but is there anything I can do? Do you need medical attention? I can probably arrange for you to see a counsellor if you like.'

She shook her head. 'Can you sort out

protection?' she asked.

'Protection?' I repeated. 'For you?'

'No,' she said. 'There's been talk, at school. Girls say they got their eye on Tia now.'

'Tia?' I was lost.

'My sister. People are saying Miles and the others are coming after Tia next.' She stopped, and for the first time I thought perhaps she might be close to tears. 'Miss Flint, you have to do something,' she said. 'She only twelve.'

# 12

I said goodbye to Rona and walked back to the station, knowing I was probably as powerless to protect Tia as Rona was.

The official line from Scotland Yard is that all reported rapes and sexual crimes are taken seriously. Spokesmen point to millions of taxpayers' money invested in the Sapphire Units. The truth is they are failing and all over London young women and girls are being let down. Because those in a position to address the problem simply dare not confront its true nature.

What the official reports and even most newspaper coverage will not say is that gang rape is endemic among young black communities. It's not the sort of thing people want to hear, but the number of reported cases goes way beyond what demographics can explain.

The girls themselves believe nothing can be done. They hate the fear they live in daily, but know they are powerless to protect themselves against these boys. And they certainly know that no one, not the police, nor their communities, not even their parents, will act or speak to help them.

And what was I going to do about it? I honestly didn't know. Yet.

Detectives operate a skeleton staff at weekends and I was expecting to find my room at Southwark police station empty. To my surprise, DC Pete Stenning was there, leaning against my desk, cheeky grin turned up to maximum. Stenning and I worked in the same team for just over a year before he'd finished his training and successfully applied to join the MIT at Lewisham. He wasn't a friend — I don't make friends at work — but we were on friendly enough terms. Normally, I wouldn't be sorry to see him, but I had a feeling this wasn't a social visit.

'I was just about to put out a call for you,' he said, as I walked over. 'You're wanted at Lewisham.'

'Have they identified the victim yet?' I asked, as Stenning drove us away from the station.

He glanced over. 'I had very clear instructions not to talk to you about the case,' he told me. 'DI Joesbury was at pains to remind me that you're a witness, not an investigating officer.'

It made sense and there was no reason for me to be pissed off. Except I really hadn't liked DI Joesbury.

'He's still around then?' I asked, wondering if the real problem had been that DI Joesbury hadn't seemed to like me.

Stenning must have picked up something in my tone. I saw him smiling to himself. 'You remember that drug ring we busted a couple of weeks ago?' he said.

I did. Sixteen million pounds' worth of heroin taken off the streets and nearly a dozen people arrested and charged. Three of them major players.

'He was a big part of it for six months,' said Stenning. 'Spent nearly a year before that just working his way into the organization. Almost got himself killed when the arrest went down.'

Well, thank heaven we were spared that loss, I thought. 'So, the victim, who is she?'

Stenning was still smiling. 'Rearrange this sentence,' he said. 'Sealed. Lips. My. Are.'

'Don't make me read it in the papers,' I pleaded.

'My instructions are to drop you off and

then get back to the estate,' he said. 'We have to knock on every door, see if anyone saw or heard anything. It's going to take days.'

Stenning was making an effort to look bored, but not really managing it. He was fired up, eager to drop me off and get out. Even in inner London, the opportunity to work on a murder investigation didn't come along every day.

'Have they had the post-mortem?' I asked, because it was worth one last try.

Stenning could turn his grin on and off like a light. 'You don't give up, do you?'

'This will all be public information in a matter of hours.'

'OK, OK. They had the PM first thing this morning,' he said. 'The DI was there. The full report won't be in for a while, but time of death fits with everything you told us and the cause was extensive blood loss. Still no clue as to who she was. No one's been reported missing. They're going to put her picture on the news tonight, see if anyone comes forward. Happy now?'

'They're putting a photograph of a corpse on national television?' I asked in disbelief, imagining a horror-struck family seeing their mother with her throat cut.

'Not a photograph, bozo, a drawing.

There's an artist over at the mortuary now working on it,' replied Stenning.

He turned into Lewisham's station car park. 'She was wearing thousands of pounds' worth of jewellery and had cash in her bag, so it wasn't about robbery. It all hinges on who she was, according to the DI. We find that out, and what she was doing on the Brendon Estate, and it should become obvious why she was killed. Everyone seems to think it'll be wrapped up pretty quickly. Oh, and there's something odd about the murder weapon, but Tulloch was keeping that pretty close to her chest.'

The room where Dana Tulloch's murder-investigation team was based was already crowded. I stopped at the open door, not quite having the nerve to go in. Tulloch had arranged for a street map of the area to be projected on to a white screen at the far end of the room. She was standing in front of it and a dozen people were grouped around her, some sitting, others leaning against desks. Then I realized that someone at the back of the room had turned to face me. Suntanned skin, turquoise eyes, one of them bloodshot. And my day was complete.

# 13

A couple of minutes later, Tulloch brought the meeting to a close. People began drifting out, one or two nodding to me. Gayle Mizon paused in the act of biting on an apple to give me a smile.

'Lacey, how are you?' Tulloch beckoned me inside. She indicated a seat and then sat down herself. She looked tired. There were shadows under her eyes and her make-up had all but disappeared. Joesbury perched himself on the desk behind her with a proprietorial air.

'I'm fine, thank you,' I said, thinking that if I concentrated on Tulloch, I wouldn't be tempted to raise my eyes a few inches and look at the man directly behind.

'Sleep well?' asked Joesbury. We both ignored him.

'Lacey, I've put in a request to have you transferred to one of the other stations until this investigation is over,' said Tulloch. 'One north of the river. I know it —'

'What?' I said, before correcting myself. 'I'm sorry, ma'am, but surely that's not —'

'Call me Dana,' she interrupted, 'and I'm afraid it is necessary. You're an important witness and if the wrong person saw you last night, I want you well out of the way.'

'I can't leave Southwark,' I said. 'That witness I was telling you about, she came in this morning. I'm just getting closer to her. I may be able to persuade her to press charges.'

There was the tiniest glint in her eyes. 'We'll make sure someone takes over . . .' she began.

'But she trusts me,' I said, making an effort not to talk too quickly. 'Or at least, she's starting to. She's seriously scared. If I leave now she'll think I've run out on her.'

Tulloch sighed. 'I understand how you feel, but last night's murder has to take priority.'

I should just agree. It made no real difference to me what station I worked from. Besides, I was low-profile girl, I didn't rock boats. 'She was raped by five boys,' I said. 'She thinks they're going after her twelve-year-old sister next. Her mother is out of her head on drugs most of the time and these girls have no one to look out for them.'

Those green eyes suddenly looked a whole lot colder. 'The decision's made, Flint,' she said. 'Deal with it.' She stood up and turned away from me. I watched her walk halfway across the room.

'Hold up a sec, Tully. Why doesn't she come here?'

Tulloch stopped and turned round. 'What?' she said.

'Bring her here,' said Joesbury, talking over my head. 'She'll be close enough to Southwark to stay with her current cases.'

Tulloch looked at him like he was simple. 'I can't have her near the investigation,' she said. 'Her credibility in court will be completely undermined if it comes out that —'

'If a detective on your team had arrived before your victim died, you'd have exactly the same issues with him,' said Joesbury. 'Keep her at arm's length, if you have to,' he went on. 'But you're going to want her on hand. She needs to go through the CCTV footage, for one thing.'

Tulloch frowned at him. A muscle beneath her left eye was flickering. 'That will take hours, at most,' she said.

'If you go ahead with the reconstruction, she'll be involved in that.'

'Yes, but —'

'You need to make sure she gets trauma

counselling, unless you want the Met to face a personal-injury claim. Much easier to see that happens if she's here.'

Tulloch stared at him for a moment, then said, 'Mark, can I talk to you for a second?'

He stood and started to follow her out of the room, before stopping and looking down at me. He took his time, taking in my lace-up brogues, pale chinos that I always wore a little too big, and the loose white shirt. My hair, as usual, was tied back at the nape of my neck and plaited. I wore my dark-rimmed glasses. No make-up or jewellery. Exactly how I always look at work.

'You certainly scrub up well,' he said at last.

'Mark!' Tulloch was at the end of her patience with both of us. Without another word, he joined her and they left the room.

I gave them a two-minute head start and then followed. I was feeling the need for caffeine. I walked the length of the corridor towards the drinks machine at the far end. I stopped just before I reached it.

The deep voice with its distinctive south London accent had already become unpleasantly familiar. Joesbury was feet away, just out of sight around the corner. 'All I'm saying is, keep an eye on her,' he said. 'You can do that a lot better if she's close. And let me make a few discreet inquiries.'

'And this has nothing to do with the fact that she's gor—'

Joesbury didn't let Tulloch finish. 'Let's just say my spider sense is tingling,' he said, in a voice I could barely hear above the gurgling of the drinks machine. 'Indulge me on this, sweetheart, OK?'

Back in the incident room, I sat alone, waiting. If I transferred to Lewisham I could stay in contact with Rona and her friends on the estate, and I'd get to see how the murder investigation panned out. The woman had died holding my hand. I couldn't help but be curious. On the other hand, I didn't really want to be surrounded by people who knew how badly I'd screwed up last night. And I still wasn't sure what to make of Joesbury and his antics.

I moved to a desk and, using a remote access password, opened up the Met's website and keyed in SO10.

Which was no longer SO10, I learned, but had been renamed the Specialist Crime Directorate, or SCD10 for short. Informally and colloquially, though, SO10 had stuck. I read that it had been formed in the 1960s to collect information on organized crime and prominent criminals. Due to advances in technology, the website claimed, the command had become a recognized world leader in covert policing methods.

So, I'd attracted the attention of a senior officer from a division with a worldwide reputation for specialist investigative techniques. Well, wasn't that a result?

After an hour, one of Tulloch's team, a good-looking black bloke in his late twenties who introduced himself as Tom Barrett, asked me to come and look at the CCTV footage from the murder site. Barrett and I crossed the small inner courtyard to another wing of the station and a tiny windowless room with a TV screen. For the next three hours I watched seemingly endless recordings of people and traffic around the estate where the murder had taken place. I saw myself, driving my black Golf along the Camberwell New Road and turning off towards the car park.

'What's that?' I asked a few minutes later. Thirty minutes or so after I drove my car into the car park, another vehicle — one decidedly out of place on an inner London council estate — went the same way.

'We've already spotted that,' replied Barrett, glancing down at some scribbled notes.

'It's a Lexus LS 460, Tuscan Olive in colour, retails at upwards of sixty grand. We can only make out the last couple of letters on the registration so it'll take time to track it down, but it's definitely of interest.'

'It's the sort of car she would have driven,' I said.

Barrett agreed with me and we got back to work. By three o'clock I was ready to slit my own wrists. There had been nothing, absolutely nothing out of the ordinary and I wasn't sure quite what we'd expected. A wild-eyed madman, perhaps dripping with blood, staggering down Camberwell New Road?

At ten past four we watched the last recording and I had a sense of freedom looming. I'd go home, draw the blinds, put on a film and curl up on the sofa. If I was lucky, I wouldn't wake till morning.

It wasn't to be. We hadn't even switched the machine off when the door opened to reveal Tulloch, a blue cotton trench coat loose around her shoulders. This time, she was alone. She nodded at Barrett and then turned to me. 'Looks like I'm stuck with you, Flint,' she said. 'You're based here until further notice and you'll bring your ongoing projects from Southwark with you.

Come on, I'll give you a lift home. We can talk on the way.'

# 14

'We've found the victim's car,' Tulloch told me as we pulled out of the car park.

'The Lexus?' I asked.

She nodded. 'We'll keep it under surveillance for a couple of days,' she said.

It was standard procedure. Plain-clothes officers would watch the car, see if anyone approached it. Anyone who showed a particular interest could well have some bearing on why the woman had been in that part of London. On the other hand . . .

'Sixty grand's worth of luxury vehicle on that estate won't go unnoticed for very long,' I said.

'Probably not,' agreed Tulloch. 'We found the keys as well. Behind a wall not far from where you found her.'

'So how . . . ?' I began.

'We think whoever killed her took the keys, meaning to drive away in her car,' said Tulloch. 'The dogs tracked someone to the alley you emerged from, but then he backtracked.'

'He heard me coming,' I said.

'Makes sense,' said Tulloch. 'You'd cut off his escape route so he had to change his plans. He ditched the keys, ran further down the block, round the rear of the buildings and made for the A3. The dogs lost him at Kennington Tube.'

'You must know who she is by now,' I said. 'The car would have been registered.'

She nodded. 'We have a pretty good idea.'

I waited. 'Are you allowed to tell me?' I asked, after a moment.

Tulloch sighed. 'It'll probably be on the news tonight,' she said. 'The car was registered to a Mr David Jones. Lives in Chiswick, married to Geraldine. We've got officers round there already, but only the au pair's at home. I'm on my way over now.'

Geraldine Jones. The name meant absolutely nothing. 'Can I come?' I found myself asking.

'Absolutely not,' she replied, glancing sideways at me. 'You should try and get some rest. You look like you need it.'

I couldn't argue with her on that one. We were silent for a while. There was something I wanted to say to her, I just didn't know how to start. So she drove and I looked at my fingernails. When I glanced up again, we were on the Wandsworth Road, not far from my flat.

'I heard there was something unusual about the murder weapon,' I said, knowing I was chancing my luck.

'That will definitely not be on the news tonight,' she replied, with a tiny half-smile as she turned into my road and pulled up against the kerb. I put my hand on the door handle and opened the door. Now or never.

'I'm sorry I screwed up,' I said. 'I know if I'd had my wits about me, she probably wouldn't have died.'

Tulloch took both hands off the wheel and twisted round in her seat to face me properly. 'What are you talking about?' she said.

'If I'd seen the attack, I could have stopped it,' I said. 'Even if it was too late for that, I could have identified who did it.'

She nodded her head slowly. 'Yes, that's possible,' she said. 'Or I might have two dead women on my hands right now and Southwark would have lost an officer.'

She turned the ignition key and the engine died. 'In any case,' she went on, 'the dogs tracked the killer to the alleyway you came out of, remember? He heard you coming and backtracked. He'd killed her and left her to die before you got anywhere near.'

She was right. I hadn't thought of that. Oh thank God.

'Lacey, you're not responsible for what happened to Geraldine Jones,' Tulloch went on. 'If that's what's been going through your head, forget it. And get some rest.'

It hadn't been my fault. Geraldine Jones hadn't died because of me. I got out of the car and thanked Tulloch for the lift. She told me to turn up at Lewisham first thing on Monday morning and drove away the minute I closed the car door. I watched the silver Mercedes turn on to the main road and felt strangely left out.

Nothing I could do. I was a witness, not an investigating officer, and finally I was home. Tulloch was right, I should rest.

But all around me life was going on and the evening was filled with that golden light September is so often blessed with. It really wasn't an evening for staying at home alone. Even if you were me. I went inside and jumped in the shower. Thirty minutes later I was on my way out, determined to make up for lost time.

Or maybe not. The top step leading down to my basement didn't normally have a scruffy-looking girl in a pink jacket standing on it, as though she couldn't quite make up her mind whether to approach my door or not. She started when I appeared, then moved back and waited for me to join her at pavement level.

'Lacey,' she said, to my surprise, because I knew I'd never seen her before. 'Can I have a word? About the murder last night? There's something you really need to know.'

# 15

'Do I know you?' I asked.

The girl was in her early twenties and, whilst I don't like myself for saying this, not the sort of person it's easy to look at. Her dyed black hair was slicked back with some greasy-looking substance and she'd tried, and failed, to cover a crop of spots around her chin with too much make-up. I counted six studs in her left ear. She didn't have a right ear. The burns scars around her lower jaw and the right side of her neck were dreadful.

'I'm Emma Boston,' she said, in a voice that might have belonged to an elderly smoker. 'I'm working on last night's murder. I've got information for you. Can we go inside?'

'What do you mean, you're working on the case?' I asked, trying to remember if I'd seen her at Lewisham or even Southwark.

Boston was wearing large sunglasses, the

sort that make it impossible to see the eyes behind them. I wondered if her eyes had suffered fire damage too. 'You were the one who found her,' she was saying. 'I heard she was still alive. Is that true?'

This woman wasn't a police officer. 'I'm going to ask you one more time, then I'm going to ask you to get off my step. What exactly are you doing here?'

Boston was about to respond when she broke into a fit of coughing. 'Did she say anything before she died?' she managed, when she got her breath back. 'Do you know who she is yet?'

Light dawned. 'Are you a reporter?' I asked.

Her lips hardened. She was used to people not responding well to her. 'Look, we both have jobs to do,' she said. 'I just think we can help each other.' She looked round the street. 'Is there somewhere we can talk?' she went on. 'I really do have some information.'

'Detective Inspector Tulloch is heading up the investigation,' I said. 'She's based at Lewisham police station.'

'OK,' she said. 'But I've had a letter that could be from the killer, and seeing as how it mentions you by name, I thought you'd be interested. My mistake.'

She pushed past me and walked up the

street towards Wandsworth Road. I watched her go, fairly sure she was lying, but . . .

I caught up with her ten metres from the corner. 'I'm sorry,' I said. 'It's been a long day.'

The lips relaxed and she glanced towards the pub on the corner. 'Want to buy me a drink?' she asked.

It was Saturday night and the pub was busy, but we went out into the beer garden and found an empty stretch of wall to lean against. Boston pulled a pack of cigarettes out of her pocket and lit one. I sipped my Diet Coke and waited. She coughed again and caught me looking at the packet.

'I shouldn't smoke,' she said, 'but my lungs are fucked up anyway, so I figure, what's the difference?'

'I'm sorry,' I said. Everything was relative. My life wasn't much to write home about, but it would be a whole lot worse if I looked like she did.

'Anything you tell me can be off the record,' she said, when she'd drawn deeply on her cigarette. 'I wouldn't quote you or anything.'

'I understand,' I said, knowing officers lost their jobs and their reputations for talking off the record to the press. Emma Boston hadn't taken out a notepad and I wondered if she was recording the conversation. She'd placed a scuffed canvas bag very close to me. 'But it sounds like you know more than I do right now,' I went on. 'I'm not part of the investigation.'

'But you found her?'

I nodded.

'Did she say anything?'

'You said you had a letter?' I asked. I couldn't afford to tell Boston more than I should because I felt sorry for her. 'A letter that mentioned me,' I went on. 'If that was a trick to get me here, I'm going home now.'

She reached into her bag and took out a thin, clear plastic folder with paper inside.

'No one's touched it but me,' she said. 'I didn't realize what it was till I pulled it from the envelope, but then I put it in a folder straight away. That was the right thing to do, wasn't it?' She seemed to want my approval now.

'Was it posted?' I asked.

She shook her head. 'No. It was pushed through the door of my house sometime last night. I found it this morning.'

'Can I see it?'

She handed it over. Inside the plastic was a sheet of fawn-coloured paper, the standard size for personal stationery. It had been folded down the middle lengthways and then twice horizontally. The fold marks were quite distinct. The handwriting was neat and legible. In red ink. There was something disturbingly familiar about it. I read it quickly. Before I was halfway through, I could feel a tingling in my cheeks.

Dear Miss Bosston

I keep on hearing Saucy Jacky is back. How I have laughed. Is it true? If it is, I hope the police are clever and on the right track.

Ask DC Flint for me — did the lady squeal? No time to clip her ears but plenty more time for funny little games.

Yours truly

A f(r)iend

Hope you like the proper red stuff.

I handed it back. 'It's gibberish,' I said. 'Some nutter's idea of a joke.'

Boston inclined her head, as though behind the dark sunglasses she was looking at me more closely. 'Are you sure?' she asked. 'You've gone very pale.'

I made a mental note that Boston probably shouldn't be underestimated.

'Actually, a joke is what I thought at first,' she went on. 'But then I found out you were with her when she died and it made me think twice. Not many people would know that.'

I was more bothered than I wanted to admit that my name was being bandied about by people I didn't know. But not nearly as bothered as I was that I knew I'd seen that letter, or something very like it, before. 'Well, if you found it out, it can't have been that hard,' I said, playing for time.

'We listen in to police radio transmissions,' she said, as if daring me to object. 'My boyfriend made a recording of last night's activity. Most people don't have the equipment to do that. But what really rung a bell with me was that reference to Saucy Jacky.'

I took it back and read the first couple of lines again. *Dear Miss Bosston, I keep on hearing Saucy Jacky is back. How I have laughed.*

'Who's Saucy Jacky?' I asked, as two things happened at once. My mobile beeped, letting me know I had a text message, and I remembered who Saucy Jacky was.

'Try Googling it,' Boston was saying. 'You'll find thousands of references. Saucy Jacky is one of the nicknames given to —'

'Jack the Ripper,' I finished for her. 'He called himself Saucy Jacky, didn't he? In letters he sent to the police.'

'And to the press,' said Boston, as I realized I was staring at her rather too hard. I pulled my phone out of my bag. The text was from Pete Stenning, letting me know that he and some of the others were heading to the Nag's Head in Peckham if I wanted to join them. Seeing me twice in twenty-four hours must have made him think of old times. Maybe he'd forgotten I'd never once accepted an invitation to go drinking with him.

'I know very little about Jack the Ripper,' I said, not sure why I was lying. 'Didn't he kill prostitutes?'

'Yes, he did,' Boston replied. 'A lot of them. Generally speaking, he cut their throats and then mutilated their abdomens. Just like what happened to that woman on Friday night. His first victim, a woman called Polly Nichols, was on 31 August 1888, but there were others after that. I think you might have a copycat on your hands.'

'Can I keep this?' I asked, indicating the letter.

'What can you tell me in return?' she replied.

I shook my head.

'No, then,' she said.

I held the letter out for her to take, and

realized my hand was shaking. 'I'll look into what you've told me,' I said. 'I'll do it tonight. And if I think it stacks up, I'll arrange for you to meet with DI Tulloch. It'll be up to her what she tells you, but if you hold off publishing anything until you've seen her, she'll be much more likely to cooperate.'

Boston was carefully putting the plastic folder back into the envelope. 'I need to meet her tomorrow,' she said, 'or I'm running with this.'

'Do you have access to scanning equipment?' I asked. When she nodded, I scribbled down my email address at work and gave it to her. I had to hope it would automatically be re-routed to Lewisham. 'Scan it and send it to me,' I said. 'And don't let anyone else touch the original. Now, how can I get in touch with you tomorrow?'

Boston wrote down her address and phone numbers for me. I took a last sip of Coke and left the pub. I went home, and some dozen years back in time.